RED FOX

To Keith, Luke, and Joe
with love

First published in the United States 1991
by Dial Books for Young Readers
A Division of Penguin Books USA Inc.
375 Hudson Street
New York, New York 10014

Published in Great Britain
by Frances Lincoln Limited
Copyright © 1991 by Hannah Giffard
Printed in Hong Kong
First Edition
1 3 5 7 9 10 8 6 4 2

Library of Congress Cataloging in Publication Data
Giffard, Hannah.
Red fox / story and pictures by Hannah Giffard.
p. cm.
Summary: Red Fox searches all night long for food
for himself and his mate, and returns to find a
happy surprise in his den.
ISBN 0-8037-0869-6
[1. Red fox—Fiction. 2. Foxes—Fiction.] I. Title.
PZ7.G3627Re   1991   [E]—dc20   90-2807   CIP   AC

RED FOX

◆ **Story and pictures by Hannah Giffard** ◆

Dial Books for Young Readers New York

The sun was setting over the faraway hills. Red Fox woke up inside the den and stretched. Rose, his mate, got up more slowly. She had slept all day, but she still felt tired. Tired and hungry.

"Stay here and rest," Red Fox told her. "I'll find us something special to eat."
Then he slipped out into the dusk.

Red Fox headed for the farm. There are always fat chickens in the barnyard, he thought. He trotted in, but stopped suddenly.

A large and very angry guard dog faced him—not at all what a red fox likes to meet.

Red Fox ran off toward the pond, leaving the barking dog behind. "There are always juicy green frogs in the reeds," he said to himself.

But tonight there were only tadpoles and an eel—not at all what a red fox likes to eat.

He heard a faint rustling in the wheat field nearby. Could it be a field mouse?

But when he parted the tall wheat there were only grasshoppers and crickets—not at all what a red fox likes to eat.

The sky was dark behind the glowing moon and Red Fox was worried. It never took this long to find food when Rose was with him. Then he heard something move . . .

His ears pricked up and he sprang toward the noise. Out of the trees popped a rabbit. He ran like the wind across the fields. Red Fox chased him to the railroad track.

He was almost close enough to touch the rabbit when a fast train came roaring around the bend.

The rabbit leaped ahead and raced up the bank. Red Fox had lost him.

Tired and thirsty, Red Fox went down to the river. He dipped his nose in the cool water, and as he drank he was amazed to see lights in the water. They were reflections from the nearby town.

Red Fox had never been to the town before. It had always been too frightening. But tonight he was desperate.

He moved through
the streets, hiding
in the shadows.
   The huge buildings
seemed to hang
in the sky above him.

Red Fox turned a corner and found himself in a narrow lane.
He watched a woman come out from a doorway.

She threw a paper bag into the trash can and went back inside.
Red Fox's nose began to twitch. What a wonderful smell!

Red Fox nudged the lid off the trash can. Then he jumped right in. The next minute he was racing off with the bag in his mouth.

As he hurried back home, the sun was shining its first beams of the day.

Red Fox entered
the dark den. Then
he paused. He could
hear squeaking and
scuffling.

As his eyes got used to the dark, he saw five little fox cubs lying next to Rose.

Red Fox beamed happily and put the bag down beside them.

Out rolled some hamburgers and fries. "Oh, Red Fox! It looks delicious," said Rose, smiling.

Together they ate every last piece.

After supper the new fox family curled up together and slept
until a new dusk.